Barkley Come Home

by Marilyn D. Anderson

illustrated by
Estella Lee Hickman

In memory of Pete,
and dedicated to the staff
at Clark Animal Hospital, Bedford, Indiana.

Published by Willowisp Press, Inc.
401 E. Wilson Bridge Road, Worthington, Ohio 43085

Printed in the United States of America

10 9 8 7 6 5 4 3

ISBN 0-87406-027-3

One

BARKLEY Boggs didn't know that June sixth was going to be a terrible day. Oh, he had noticed his family putting a lot of stuff in boxes, and his master Jamie Boggs had tried to warn him. But the whiskery-faced part-Schnauzer still didn't understand. He never guessed that his happy days on Elm Street were about to end.

That day Barkley went out for his usual morning walk. He chased the same rabbit out of the flower bed that he always did. He rounded up all the neighbors' squirrels as usual. Then he headed on down the street for his daily inspection of smells.

Suddenly a huge, blue truck roared around the corner, hogging the whole road and nearly hitting

Barkley. The driver had the nerve to blow his horn, which made the Schnauzer furious. From the safety of the curb, he barked angrily until the truck retreated. Then, proud of his victory, the dog went on with his business.

Everything else on Elm Street seemed to be in order. Before very long, Barkley set off for home at a swinging trot. His mind was on breakfast. He could almost taste the cup of meaty brown nuggets that would be waiting for him. Jamie would say, "Want some chow?" and he would tilt his head back to one side and his right ear would stand up. He'd raise his right paw and bark just once as if to say, "Yes." Then Jamie would say, "Good dog," and he'd pour the food into the dish. Yum.

But as Barkley reached his house, he saw the same truck he'd tangled with earlier parked in his driveway. He rushed forward, barking and growling.

"Barkley, be quiet," Mr. Boggs called out the window. "Jamie, you'd better tie up your dog before he bothers the movers."

Immediately the boy hurried out with a rope to catch his dog, but Barkley saw him coming. Eyes flashing and tail wagging, Barkley dashed away. If there was one thing he liked better than breakfast, it was a good game of tag.

"Barkley, come here," Jamie ordered. "This is no time for silliness." The tone of Jamie's voice took the starch out of the Schnauzer's tail very quickly. In fact, he nearly dropped to his belly trying to apologize.

Now it was the boy's turn to feel bad. "I'm sorry I yelled at you," he said, giving the dog a big hug. "I'd like to play, I really would, but we're moving."

Barkley felt better then. He tried to lick Jamie's face and to sit as close to his boy as possible. He wanted to be petted and thought maybe they'd play tag after all.

"Jamie," Mrs. Boggs called. "You mustn't take all day with that dog. Now please tie him up so you can help me."

The boy sighed as he fastened Barkley's rope to a tree. When Jamie left, the dog got very upset. He hadn't done anything wrong, he knew. It was just that the truck was unfamiliar. He circled around and around the tree. His rope got shorter and shorter. Soon he was wedged tight against the tree.

Jamie reappeared, carrying Barkley's dish. "You silly dog," he said, putting the food on the ground. "You've got to settle down." The boy unwound the rope while the grateful dog tried to lick him to death. "Here's your breakfast. Now eat it," Jamie said.

The Schnauzer looked at the food and then at Jamie. He wasn't interested in eating anymore. Besides, the boy hadn't even asked him if he wanted it. Barkley could feel an excitement in the air that made him want to prance and whine.

"It's all right, fella," Jamie explained. "That truck is supposed to be here. It has to take our stuff to Indiana."

Barkley sat and studied Jamie's face more

intently. “Yes, yes, you get to go, too,” the boy assured him. Then Jamie left again.

Frustrated, the dog trotted and sat, trotted and sat. He saw two strange men come out of his house carrying the Boggs’ sofa. Trembling with excitement, he barked at them to stop, but they paid no attention to him. Nervously he used his sharp claws to tear at the grass. His front feet made the dirt fly. Barkley was almost standing on his head in the hole he’d made.

About that time Mr. Boggs came by. “Barkley!” he yelled. “Stop that! Jamie, come here and move this dog.”

Barkley looked up at Mr. Boggs with a muddy grin and wagged his tail. Would Jamie’s father set him free? he wondered. Mr. Boggs just shook his head. Jamie untied the rope.

Joyously, Barkley jumped around and tried to drag Jamie toward the house. Instead, the boy took him to the garage. The Schnauzer whined and begged when he saw he was being tied again. But it did no good.

"Maybe you can stay out of trouble here," said Jamie as he started out the door.

Barkley got really frantic then. With strange men in his house, he just had to get loose. He tugged and fought the rope, leaping into the air in his desperation. Finally he saw that it was hopeless, so he flopped in a miserable heap. He felt like chewing on something. There was only one thing close by.

It took Barkley a long time for his teeth to work their way through the rope. It took even longer for him to realize he was free. Then he rushed to look out the door. Seeing no one, he slipped into the bushes that lined the walk. One of the strangers was carrying Jamie's bicycle, and the dog followed. Staying behind the hedge, he kept out of sight until the bike was on the truck. The stranger returned to the house.

Barkley went to examine the truck more closely, and what he saw troubled him. Everything the Boggs family owned was on board. If they were going somewhere, he didn't want to be left behind. Carefully he slipped under Jamie's bike and found a hiding spot. He crouched low when he heard someone coming.

"Hey, not so fast," complained a man wearing old tennis shoes. "This chest is heavy."

"Quit your griping. It's not that bad," said a pair of brown boots.

Barkley flattened himself lower and froze. He was well hidden except for one small problem. His tail was still in plain sight. Minutes later one of the men stepped on it.

With a yelp of pain Barkley pulled in his bruised tail. The moving man yelped as he fought to keep his balance and failed. The man and the chest fell with a loud crack of splitting wood.

"You clumsy oaf," shouted the brown boots. "You've knocked off one of the legs."

"It wasn't my fault. There aren't supposed to be any dogs on the truck."

"Dogs? Hey, get out of there, you mutt."

Barkley cowered under pieces of furniture and tried to become invisible.

"Guess I'd better get the owner," the brown boots continued. "You keep an eye on him while I'm gone."

Jamie and his father came at once. Mr. Boggs was furious with Barkley. "You're a real nuisance today," he stormed. "Come on out."

The dog cringed and shifted his feet. He was too frightened to show his face.

"Jamie, crawl in there and drag him out," Mr. Boggs ordered.

The boy got down on all fours and started toward the dog. "Come on, fella," he coaxed. "You can't stay here. Dad's got enough problems today without you acting up."

Barkley held himself rigid so that Jamie couldn't budge him. The boy refused to give up. They struggled until Jamie succeeded. Mr. Boggs snapped a leash on the dog.

"Now then," said Jamie's father, handing him the leash, "don't let Barkley out of your sight until we're ready to leave."

"That's good advice," said one of the movers.

"We wouldn't want to lock up your dog with the load."

"What would happen to him if you did?" Jamie asked.

The man shrugged. "Well, look at it this way. This truck won't get to Indiana for a couple of days, and we don't feed pets along the way."

Jamie thought about that for a moment. Then he said, "Gee, I hope they feed pets on the airplane."

Mr. Boggs said, "At the prices they charge, they'd better."

"Why can't we just take him in the car? It would be lots cheaper," Jamie said.

"Son, we've been through that. It's going to be a long, hot trip. We'd have to make stops along the way. He'd be a terrible problem," Mr. Boggs said. He put his arms around Jamie's shoulders.

"Maybe you're right," the boy admitted. "But I sure hate sending him off by himself." Jamie shook his head. He bent down to pet Barkley. The dog licked Jamie's fingertips.

Two

A few hours later the Boggs family was having a final look at their house on Elm Street. Jamie said sadly, "Too bad Mike's at camp. I can't even tell him good-bye."

Jamie's mother put her hand on her son's shoulder. "I think it's better this way," she said softly.

"I hate good-byes," his father agreed. "They only make everyone feel sad." He didn't say anything else for a few minutes. At last he opened the car and announced, "Barkley is due at the airport in an hour. Let's get going."

Immediately the dog leaped in. He was so happy to be invited along that he bounded from the front seat to the backseat. There he ran from side to side, pressing his nose against one window and then another.

Mr. Boggs sighed as he climbed into the driver's seat. "And you wanted to take him all the way to Indiana in the car. Thank heavens I vetoed that," he said.

Barkley kept his nose planted against the car window for a while. Then he flopped down on the seat with his head in Jamie's lap. The boy stroked the Schnauzer's rough coat and said, "You're going on a long trip, fella. I won't be able to see you for a while, but I'll be thinking about you."

The dog licked Jamie's face and grunted happily. "I hope you won't mind staying in that cage," the boy added.

Catching the note of concern in Jamie's voice, Barkley looked up, wondering. But he couldn't guess what the words meant.

* * * * *

The Schnauzer hated the airport from the beginning. When Mr. Boggs stopped the car outside the main building and got out, Barkley decided he'd stay where he was. Unfortunately Jamie wouldn't let him do that. Instead, the dog was dragged out into the noisy crowds and confusion. He leaned hard against the boy's legs for reassurance.

"It's okay, Barkley. Really, it is," Jamie told him.

Mr. Boggs took a big cage with wire windows from the trunk of the car. He put it on the sidewalk. People stared and walked around him. "Son, it's time," he said softly.

"Do we have to?" Jamie pleaded.

"Yes, this is best for everyone," his father said firmly. "The next two days aren't going to be much fun for any of us, I'm afraid."

When they tried to bring Barkley to the cage, he pulled back as hard as he could. He pushed his feet against the sides of the cage, straining not to be shoved in. But Jamie, his mom and dad were too much for him. As the door closed, Barkley whined and scratched at the sides.

"He doesn't like it in there," Jamie said worriedly.

"I didn't think he would," said Mr. Boggs. "But he'll settle down after a while. Did you bring his food?"

"It's right here," said Mrs. Boggs, holding up a paper bag. "Now, how are we going to get that big cage to the baggage room?"

"May I help you?" asked a voice at her elbow. They looked around to see a big man with bushy eyebrows standing behind her. He wore a uniform, and he stood next to something that looked like a golf cart. "I could take the cage for you," he said.

Mr. Boggs nodded. "Yes, please do," he agreed. "I'll park the car and meet you in a few minutes."

"All right, sir," said the big man, lifting Barkley's cage onto his cart. Frantically the dog scrambled from side to side, rocking the cage.

"Please be careful," Jamie begged. "My dog is pretty scared." The man in the uniform nodded. Jamie and Mrs. Boggs climbed into the cart. Mr. Boggs left in the car.

The cart took them right through the automatic doors and into a big glass building. They went down a long hall packed with people who stared. The dog crouched down in the cage. Next, the cart drove onto an elevator. As they dropped down, Barkley braced himself, wondering what would happen next.

"It's all right, Barkley. It's all right," Jamie kept repeating.

At last the cart stopped. The driver carried the cage into a room. A woman sat behind a high counter. "May I help you?" the lady asked.

"Yes, we want to ship Barkley, our dog, to Indianapolis," said Mrs. Boggs.

"Oh, sure," said the lady, smiling. "Just fill out these papers, and I'll take care of everything." Mr. Boggs arrived as Mrs. Boggs finished filling out the papers. "Thank you," said the lady.

JAMIE

"Now, would you bring your dog this way?"

The big man lifted the cage once more. Barkley was taken into a room where several other cages sat. Mrs. Boggs handed over the bag of dog food while Mr. Boggs paid the man in the uniform.

"I think we have everything we need," said the lady. "Want to tell your dog good-bye?"

Jamie nodded as tears welled up in his eyes. He got down on his knees, and reached his fingers through the wires at the side of the cage. His dog licked them. "Good-bye, Barkley. We'll see you in a few days," he sniffed. Then Jamie and his parents left.

Barkley was horrified. Jamie couldn't be leaving him here alone, he thought. He barked, howled, and he whimpered. But Jamie didn't come back.

There were dogs in some of the other cages. None of them, however, seemed interested in Barkley's problem. All Barkley could do was lie down and wait.

Several hours later the door burst open.

Barkley got to his feet eagerly. Was it Jamie? he wondered. But he realized at once that the whistling young man who had come in was not his master.

"Hi, pups. How about a little grub?" the man asked cheerfully. Then, after pausing to check a clipboard, he began to dish out food. "Let's see. The poodle gets a pouch of this and vitamin pills. The Doberman gets two cups of this stuff . . . . "

As the man got closer, Barkley began to whine and wag his tail. His right ear stood up. Barkley raised his right paw. "Ruff," he said.

The man chuckled at him. "Say, you're a friendly one . . . cute, too. I'd like to let you out of there, but it's against the rules," he said.

When Barkley whined again, the man leaned down to reach inside the cage. "I like you. You've got personality," he said, scratching the dog's ears. A gold chain that hung from the man's neck rattled against the wire of the cage.

"Well," said the man, getting to his feet at last, "I'd better be going. Sleep tight, pooches." With that he shut off the light and headed out the door.

Suddenly Barkley felt so lonesome that he let out an enormous howl. The light came right back on, and the man poked his head in to look around. "Gosh, was that you?" he asked, coming over to Barkley's cage. "Would you feel better if you had a night-light?"

The dog licked the man's hand as he reached into the cage, and the man shrugged. "All right then. I won't tell if you don't," he said. When the door closed this time, the light stayed on.

The next morning a different man put Barkley's cage on a cart and wheeled him outside. Other carts zipped around them. The wind carried strange smells. Barkley's cage was placed with a large pile of suitcases. The suitcases were being shoved into something like a metal building on wheels. Would his cage be put in there, too? he wondered.

Then Barkley heard a cheerful whistle and a familiar voice. "Hi, there, pooch. Did you sleep okay last night?" the man asked.

Barkley whined and wagged his tail eagerly, hoping the man would come closer. Finally the man's blue eyes looked at him through the wire. His hand started in to pet him. The gold chain bumped against the front of the cage and got caught.

"Aw heck," the man complained, trying to pull the chain loose. Suddenly the door to Barkley's cage flew open. He started through the door, then hesitated. There was chaos on all sides. Which way should he go? he wondered.

The man scrambled toward Barkley. "Take it easy, pooch," he said desperately. "Stay right where you are. I've got to get you on that plane."

Quickly Barkley lunged away, only to look back. The man had been kind to him. Should he stay? he wondered. No, if the man put him back in that cage, he'd never get to Elm Street.

Barkley wandered off a little farther, still glancing back at the man who followed. Another man riding by on a cart just missed hitting him.

Jumping out of the way, Barkley collided with a man carrying a load of boxes. The boxes flew in all directions, and one fell under the wheels of yet another cart. That cart went crazy, dumping its load of magazines in a puddle of water. All of these men joined in chasing after Barkley.

"Get that dog. Try to corner him," they called to each other.

As the men closed in, the dog's path was barred by a group of proper-looking old men whose attention was on an approaching plane. They waved little flags and cheered, but they never noticed Barkley.

His pursuers were so close now that one of them made a grab for the dog. At that, Barkley hurtled into the group of flag wavers. He bounced off bodies and briefcases, knocking several people down.

"My word," sputtered one old gentleman, struggling to his feet. "This sort of thing would never happen on the continent."

There was a chorus of "excuse me" as the

airport workers tried to follow Barkley. But, by now, any hope they might have had of catching the dog was gone. He was in the clear and racing to find Jamie.

Three

AS Barkley got farther away from his pursuers, he began to slow down. The field he was in had several roads crossing it, and he couldn't decide which way to go. In fact, he was about to sit down to consider things when a huge machine came roaring at him from the sky. He flattened himself as the plane skimmed the top of his head and rumbled to the ground right next to him. Then he saw a second plane approaching and another one beyond that.

Quick as a flash, Barkley put his tail between his legs and galloped away. Wildly he ran toward a clump of bushes at the side of the field. There, in a tangled mass of vines, he lay breathless and shaking.

When he recovered enough to notice where he was, Barkley saw that he'd landed right in the middle of a cocklebur bush. His hair was all matted and his ears wouldn't even go up. He let out a howl of frustration and pulled at the burrs with his teeth. He wanted to go home.

Barkley tried to drag himself out of the underbrush, but he found that he was stuck. Stubborn little twigs were caught in his collar. He tugged and twisted until he felt something let go. Looking up, he saw his license tags hanging from the bush. Barkley didn't care about those. He was just glad to be free.

Escaping from the underbrush at last, the dog discovered a gravel road. He followed the road and found that it curved back toward the airport and ended next to the exit gate. Just beyond the gate was a street full of stopped cars.

Now Barkley had a healthy respect for cars, but he decided to chance crossing the street. He was about half way across when the cars began to move slowly. Horns tooted. Drivers yelled at him.

Brakes squealed. It was a nightmare.

Not far ahead of Barkley was a truck with its end gate down. Desperately, the dog launched himself at the truck. He made it, only to fall hard on the slick floor.

At first Barkley was so glad to be leaving that noisy airport that he didn't even try to get up. He sensed that the truck was heading away from Elm Street. That upset him. He struggled to his feet for a look, wondering what he should do next. One glance at the fast moving pavement discouraged him from jumping. There was nothing he could do until the truck slowed down again.

Soon they were leaving the city, and Barkley saw fewer houses. He quivered with excitement at each strange, new smell. Where was he going? he wondered.

The truck went on and on at a steady pace. Finally Barkley wobbled back to a spot just behind the cab to lie down. If he couldn't do anything else, he might as well take a nap, he thought.

It was late in the day when the truck did slow down. They turned onto a new road and then another. The third road was so rough that they were barely moving.

Barkley made his way to the side of the truck and looked out. All he could see were trees, but that really didn't matter. With a mighty leap, he sailed over the side of the truck, landing in a thick clump of grass in the ditch. He wasn't hurt, just terribly lonely.

After sniffing the breeze for a few minutes, Barkley walked along the ditch and into a grove of trees. On the other side of the trees was a field where plants grew in long rows. He crawled under a fence and followed the rows. As he trotted along, he realized that he was a very long way from Elm Street. Something else was bothering him, too. Barkley was hungry.

All dogs like to hunt, but Barkley was a city dog. He had never caught anything in his life. His nose told him there were lots of small animals around. He could smell rabbits, mice, and other

animals he couldn't identify. But would he be able to catch one? he wondered.

Suddenly his sharp ears picked up the sound of something moving in the leaves. He sprang into action. A small body quivered under his feet. He reached in with his jaws to pin it to the ground. Instead he got a surprise. The tiny animal had teeth of its own, and it buried them in Barkley's tender nose. With a yelp, he leaped away to paw at his face. The small animal disappeared down a hole.

Shaken, Barkley set off again. The field was big. The sun went down before he reached another fence. Hardly anything was growing in the next field, yet a sickly sweet smell promised him that some kind of food was ahead. There was also a strong smell of an animal.

If he hadn't been so hungry, Barkley might have tried to find a safer detour. But he decided to investigate. Worming his way under the fence, he made his way toward a row of metal containers that smelled of food. He had no problem flipping the lid of one to reach inside. But, before he'd gotten a taste of the food, he heard something. He listened carefully. A series of low grunts and squeals met his ears. There was the sound of running feet.

Seconds later a herd of animals galloped toward him. Their smell was overpowering. Barkley darted behind one of the metal containers as the clumsy animals thundered by. Then, grinning to himself, he flipped a container lid to grab a big mouthful of food. The bite of dry powder almost choked him.

Barkley looked around and coughed as he heard the strange animals returning. This time he heard something else, too. Dogs and lights were coming his way. There were people yelling in the distance.

"Something's after the hogs. Get your gun," someone said.

"Our dogs will handle it. Sick 'em, dogs," another person answered.

Barkley didn't wait to hear any more. He

barreled under the nearest fence, and ran and ran.

Coming at last to a little stream, Barkley gratefully washed the last of the dry, scratchy food from his throat. Then he followed the stream until he came to an old barn. It seemed to be deserted so he decided to spend the rest of the night there. Barkley collapsed and fell asleep in a dark corner of the barn.

The next morning Barkley slept late. He had run so many miles the day before that he didn't want to move. The hay under him was soft. He could almost imagine he was back on Elm Street, almost feel Jamie's hand petting him. In his sleep, he grunted and wiggled with pleasure.

"Hi, dog," said a voice right next to his ear. "What are you doing here?"

Barkley jerked himself awake to realize there really was someone touching him. His reflexes said, "Bite! Defend yourself!" His brain told him to run.

Four

SEVERAL leaps later Barkley looked back to see a blonde-haired girl watching him. There was a confused expression on her face.

"What's the matter?" she asked gently. "I only want to pet you."

Feeling rather foolish, Barkley wagged his tail and tried to apologize. Barkley sensed she was a nice girl. He crouched down on his belly as he came forward grinning. He looked up at her from under his long eyelashes and begged her to pet him some more.

She did so eagerly. Her tiny hands tried to pull out some of his burrs. "Good dog," she told him. "I won't hurt you."

When Barkley rolled over on his back, the girl

seemed to know exactly what he wanted. She scratched his stomach and tickled him under the chin.

"Are you hungry, dog?" she asked at last. "Mama's still asleep, but I can fix you breakfast." Taking Barkley's wiggles as a "yes," she got up and started toward the house. The dog stuck to her like glue.

They went right into the kitchen where the little girl climbed up onto the counter top to reach into the cupboard. She put cereal and milk in a bowl and sprinkled sugar on the whole thing.

Barkley didn't care too much about the sugar, but the rest tasted delicious. He wolfed down the cereal and licked the bowl. Then he begged for more.

"How about some eggs?" asked his new friend. She broke several in a pan and turned on the heat.

Although she missed the pan with one egg and burned the whites a bit, Barkley wasn't about to complain. After licking the plate and the frying pan, he looked up and licked his chops.

"Still hungry?" she marveled. "Well, let's see what else I can find."

She had barely begun to look inside the refrigerator when someone started yelling. "Tracy, what are you doing? And where did you get that dirty dog?"

Barkley froze, wondering where he could hide.

Tracy pulled her head out of the refrigerator to explain. "He's my new pet, Mama. He's hungry."

"Oh, Honey," groaned the woman who stood before them in her bathrobe. "How many times have I told you that stray dogs are dangerous? And look at the mess you've made."

Then a boy about Jamie's age appeared. "What's going on?" he asked.

The woman turned to him. "Barry, just look at what your sister dragged in," she said.

"He's cute," the boy said immediately. And, offering Barkley the back of one hand to sniff, he added, "At least he would be without all those burrs."

"Can I keep him, Mama?" Tracy begged.

"Yeah, Mom, can we keep him?" echoed Barry.

The woman shook her head determinedly. "We can't keep every animal that wanders through here. Besides, he probably has an owner somewhere," she said.

"Then he shouldn't be running around this neighborhood by himself," the boy pointed out. "Somebody is likely to shoot him."

"I suppose you're right," she admitted. "After that pack of stray dogs scared those kids in South Port, folks are pretty upset."

"I think we ought to tie him up for his own good," Barry suggested.

"But I want to play with him," Tracy said.

Her mother sighed, then said, "We'll tie him up until you're both done with breakfast. Then we'll see."

Barry took Barkley outside and found an old chain. He hooked it to Barkley's collar. "Too bad he doesn't have any tags," said the boy's mother. "If he did, we'd know where he came from."

"He probably lost those wherever he picked up the burrs," said Barry. The boy fastened the dog to a tree and told him, "Be a good dog now, and maybe Mom will let you stay."

But Barkley didn't want to stay. He wanted to find Jamie. As soon as Barry was gone, he pulled hard on the chain. It held him fast. He tried gnawing the chain, but that hurt his teeth. Again there was nothing to do but wait.

When the children came out a little later, Barkley jumped around joyously. But they didn't unfasten him. Instead, Barry had brought a comb to use on the dog's burrs. When Barry tried to pull out the burrs, the Schnauzer wiggled, rolled over on his back, and moaned dramatically.

"You're a big baby," laughed Barry as he gave Barkley a pat. Then, pulling the dog to his feet, he told Tracy, "Come here and hold him for me."

Tracy bent down to grab Barkley's collar, and Barkley licked her face. "Yes, I know you like me," she giggled. "But you've got to hold still."

Barry went back to pulling the burrs out of

Barkley's hair. The dog lay down again, this time taking Tracy with him. The children pulled Barkley to his feet many more times only to have him collapse in the grass. Between all the wrestling and the doggie kisses, it took a long time to finish the grooming job. At last Barry put the comb in his pocket and said, "Okay, boy, you're done."

Barkley was so relieved that he leaped to his feet. He barked happily as he raced back and forth on the chain. It felt good to be rid of the burrs. He was delighted to find that his ears went up and down again.

Next the children took the dog to the back door for their mother's inspection. "He is sort of cute," she admitted. "And he seems to have a nice personality."

"May I take him over to Jimmy's?" asked Barry. "We're going fishing this morning."

His mother frowned. "Oh, Barry, why don't you stay here with the dog?" she asked.

"We can tie him to a tree while we fish. Jimmy's going to love him," Barry insisted.

"But I want to play with him, too," said Tracy, pouting.

Barry took a step toward Barkley. "He's going

fishing with us," he insisted.

Their mother sighed. "Tracy, what if you went with the boys? You could take along some dolls and some food and have a nice picnic," she said.

"A picnic!" Tracy bubbled eagerly. "That's a great idea. I'll get my basket."

When she had gone Barry asked angrily, "Mom, why did you have to say that? Jimmy and I don't want her along."

"I'm sorry, dear," his mother explained. "I have to shop for Tracy's birthday present this morning. If you're going fishing, so is she."

Barry made a face and shrugged.

"And I want you to keep track of her," his mother continued. "Is that clear?"

Barry frowned harder, but he nodded.

Tracy came back wearing a red hooded sweatshirt. She carried a very full wicker basket.

"What do you have in there?" her brother asked glumly.

"I'm Red Riding Hood, and I'm taking some things to my grandma," she said, smiling.

"Terrific," Barry moaned.

Jimmy liked Barkley a lot, but he was not enthusiastic about taking Tracy with them. "We'll never get to where the fish are biting if she goes along," he complained.

"My mom didn't give me a choice," Barry assured him. "Are you taking that rifle along?"

Jimmy nodded and looked a little embarrassed. "Dad said I had to take it with me whenever I'm away from the house," he said.

"How come?" Barry asked.

"Oh, you know how my father is. Some dogs bothered a kid over in South Port. He thinks I'll be their next victim."

Barry grinned, and they started off along the creek bank. At first Tracy carried her own basket. But, before long, she began to lag behind.

"This basket is too heavy," she whined. "Why do we have to go so far?"

"You take the dog, and I'll carry the basket," Barry decided.

Still the little girl failed to keep up so Barry

handed his fishing pole to Jimmy. Then he managed the basket as well as Barkley. Everyone was getting crabby by the time they came to a little grove of trees with some freshly cut stumps.

"Why don't you and the dog stay here?" Barry asked Tracy. "We can pick you up on the way back."

"When are you coming back?" she asked suspiciously.

"In a little while," Barry said.

"But where are you going?" she asked.

"Just a little further down the creek. We'll be within earshot all the time," he assured her. "We can't forget you because you've got the food."

Tracy thought about that for a minute and nodded. Then Barry fastened Barkley's chain to a tree, and the boys went off to fish. Tracy took doll clothes out of her basket, but she hadn't brought any dolls. Instead, she tried the clothes on Barkley. They were all too small except for one frilly pink bonnet which he hated.

"My, what big teeth you have, Grandma," she

giggled. After that she had to tell Barkley the entire story of *Little Red Riding Hood.* "Let's act it out," she decided. "Your bed can be right over there, but I'll have to untie you so you can reach it."

Barkley wagged his tail hopefully as Tracy unsnapped the chain from his collar. This could be his chance to escape, he thought. But, glancing around to see where he might go, the Schnauzer saw something that made him growl deep down in his throat.

Five

TRACY caught the warning in Barkley's growl and turned to stare at the strange dogs. "Oh," she said uncertainly. "Barry! Barry! Come here," she yelled.

The pack of dogs hesitated, and looked around warily. When nothing happened, they began to slink forward. The hair stood up on the back of Barkley's neck. He wanted to run or hide, but Tracy would surely be attacked if he left her alone.

"Barry!" Tracy called again. Once more the dogs hesitated.

As the pack crept closer, Barkley knew it was time to act. "Gruff," he challenged, darting near the face of the biggest dog. His unexpected move had given him a small head start. He raced off in the direction the boys had taken. Immediately he heard a snarl that told him this was one game of tag he couldn't afford to lose. At least the pack had forgotten Tracy for now.

The boys must not have heard Tracy's cries. They were still fishing when they first sighted the dogs. "Oh, my gosh," sputtered Jimmy, leaping for his rifle.

"Don't shoot," yelled Barry. "You might hit the wrong dog." So Jimmy waited until Barkley was almost on top of him and the other dogs were inches behind. "Bang," went his gun. Glancing back, Barkley saw the lead dog falter. "Bang, bang," the gun repeated, and the other dogs turned and ran.

"Creepers," Barry remembered, heading up the creek at a mad run. "I hope Tracy's all right," he yelled.

"I'm right behind you," answered Jimmy. "Come on, pooch. You don't want to tangle with those dogs again."

But Barkley didn't follow the boys. If he was going to find Jamie, he had to be free. He forded the little stream and trotted off in what he hoped was the direction of Elm Street.

* * * * *

After two days of driving, the Boggs family finally reached their new home. The moving van had not arrived, yet. But they had a stove on which to cook supper, and they slept in sleeping bags. Life seemed pretty weird to them without a TV or phone.

"I sure miss Barkley," Jamie told his father as he lay on the floor in the dark.

"I miss him, too," Mr. Boggs admitted. "But we'll pick him up in Indianapolis tomorrow."

"He's sure going to be glad to see us, huh, Dad?" Jamie said.

"Yup, he might just send himself into orbit wagging that tail of his. Good night, Son," Jamie's dad said.

The next morning the Boggs family drove to the airport. Jamie's father told the baggage clerk what they wanted. "I think you have something, or should I say someone, here that belongs to us," Mr. Boggs said, winking at Jamie.

"What sort of someone are you speaking of?" asked the very serious gentleman behind the desk.

"Barkley's a dog," Jamie piped up, "about this big with a furry face."

"I have the shipping papers right here," said his father, holding out the document for the man to see.

The man studied the forms carefully and consulted his computer. "That's odd," he muttered. "We don't have any animals back there right now."

"But the woman in Albany assured us that Barkley would be here today," said Mrs. Boggs worriedly.

"I'm checking on him," the man informed her, punching still more buttons on his machine.

"Maybe he got sent to some other airport by mistake."

"What other airport?" cried Jamie. "Where is he?"

"Calm down, Son. I'm sure we'll know in a minute or two," said Mr. Boggs.

"But Barkley's lost. We've got to find him," Jamie insisted.

The baggage man looked up and said confidently, "Not really lost, just misplaced. Have a seat and try to be patient while I try to find him."

"Bernard, I don't like the sound of this," whispered Jamie's mother as they went to sit in some padded chairs. "Where can Barkley be?"

Mr. Boggs patted his wife on the shoulder and said, "Now, Sarah, you heard the man. This sort of thing does happen. They probably sent him to Minneapolis instead of Indianapolis."

"I don't want him in Minneapolis," Jamie said unhappily. "I want him here."

"Barkley will be here," Mr. Boggs assured him.

"We just need to be patient and give the man some time to find him. Try looking at one of these magazines."

About ten minutes later, the baggage man came up to Jamie's family looking rather embarrassed. "Mr. Boggs," he began, "I'm afraid I have some bad news for you."

Jamie's father looked up from the magazine he was reading. "What kind of bad news?" he asked.

"Is it about Barkley?" Jamie asked. His magazine fell to the floor without being noticed.

"I'm afraid so," the man admitted. "It seems there was some sort of mix-up in Albany and your dog escaped."

"Escaped?" the Boggs cried in unison.

"Well, what happened to him then?" demanded Mr. Boggs. "Didn't anyone try to catch him? What's the matter with your airline?"

The man looked around unhappily. "Sir, to my knowledge this has never happened before. My airline is very careful, and they assured me that our people did try to catch the dog.

Unfortunately he disappeared before they could get hold of him."

"Oh, no, what if he got hit by a car?" howled Jamie. "What if he's lying hurt somewhere? Oh, poor Barkley!"

The baggage man looked even more unhappy. "My company will reimburse you for the full value of the dog, and may I say that I offer you our most sincere apologies . . . "

Mr. Boggs snorted at him angrily. "Save your apologies and keep your money. We want our dog. Tell your boss to send someone looking for him. Offer a reward, but find that dog!"

"Well, I'll see what we can do," sputtered the man. "This is a most unusual case."

"Here's our new phone number. The phone will be installed today," Mr. Boggs interrupted. "I'll expect to hear something from you very soon."

With that, Jamie's father turned and headed for the nearest bank of telephones. He started to dig in his wallet.

"Bernard, what are you going to do?" asked

Mrs. Boggs, catching up.

"I'm calling Mike's folks," he explained. "He should be home from camp by now, and if anybody can find a lost dog, it's a kid."

"That's a great idea, Dad," said Jamie. "Let me talk to him."

"But how do we know Barkley went back to Elm Street?" Mrs. Boggs wondered.

"We don't," Mr. Boggs admitted. "But it's the only thing I can think of right now."

Six

ABOUT the same time Jamie learned that Barkley was missing, the weary dog was crossing yet another field. He felt like he had crossed hundreds of them already. His feet were sore from traveling all night. His stomach demanded food. At the end of this field, he saw something that made him almost forget how badly he felt. Ahead was a large group of houses — a regular town.

His heart beat joyfully as Barkley scooted under a fence and across a narrow road. As he got closer to the houses, he could see sidewalks, street lights, and fire hydrants. The place looked almost like home.

Barkley lost no time in exploring the smells of

the strange town. But he hadn't gotten far when a little brown Chihuahua ran out barking. Standing at the edge of the yard, the dog's frantic barking brought answers from all directions. It also brought out an angry old woman.

"Go away, ya mangy mutt," she croaked, hurrying to help her pint-sized watch dog. "We don't like strays around here."

Barkley bent low and lengthened his stride. This certainly wasn't like Elm Street, he thought. No one yelled at him there just for walking by.

Suddenly a fierce-looking bulldog barred the sidewalk ahead. He stood alert, waiting.

Barkley made sure the street was empty and started to walk it. The bulldog took the street, too. The Schnauzer crossed to the opposite sidewalk. The other dog did, too. Barkley knew he would either have to face the bulldog or run. While he hesitated, the bulldog decided for him.

Stiffly, the big dog came forward, nostrils snorting. Barkley met him just as stiffly. Then their noses met. The bulldog moved off to one side for more sniffing, and the Schnauzer bristled. The stranger poked and prodded with his nose. Barkley turned with a low growl that said, "Watch it, Buster."

Luckily the bulldog took the warning and moved back a bit. Barkley saw his chance to escape. Bounding away, he left the slower dog outdistanced and angry. The speedy Schnauzer found himself outside the housing development. There were more fields and more groups of houses. Discouraged, Barkley remembered again how tired and hungry he was.

He was barely moving when a faint scent of food met his nose. It was the smell of hamburgers frying. It reminded him of the times he'd gone in the car to eat with Jamie. The boy always dropped a few French fries on purpose. Jamie always shared the bread around his burger.

Barkley followed his nose until he came to a little glass-sided building, just like the one he remembered. Immediately his attention was focused on a yellow school bus parked next to the building. Jamie had come home in something like that a million times. Maybe he was on the bus.

Eagerly trotting forward, Barkley watched the boys getting off. They were bigger than Jamie, and they all seemed to be wearing funny hats.

Although none of the boys looked familiar to him, several of the boys stopped to pat the Schnauzer. He wagged his tail and cocked his head to one side to show them he was friendly.

"Hi there, sport," said a redheaded boy, hurrying toward Barkley. "Are you waiting for someone?" When the other boys moved on, this boy stayed to check Barkley's collar. "Hmmm," he said to himself. "No tags, but you used to have some."

Barkley wiggled all over at the boy's touch. Then he sat down and gave the redhead his best pleading look. A man went by with a cheeseburger, and Barkley licked his chops.

"I'll bet you're hungry," the redhead decided. "Just wait here. I'll bring you something."

The Schnauzer watched intently as the boy

disappeared into the building. He figured the boy would bring food, and he was right. When the redhead returned he carried a paper bag that smelled deliciously. Several other boys who also carried bags followed. Barkley began to drool.

"See, he waited for me," the redhead told them proudly. "Let's see if he's hungry."

No sooner did a piece of bread appear than Barkley swallowed it. His bright eyes rivoted on the redhead's hands, licking his chops frantically.

"You're right, Freddy," said a chubby boy. "I'll bet he hasn't eaten in a week." Then the chubby boy handed Barkley part of a fish sandwich. There was too much mayonnaise on the fish, but he didn't complain. He downed that morsel in one gulp. Soon all the other boys were eager to offer Barkley goodies.

"You know something," Freddy said wistfully. "I've always wanted a dog like this. I wish I could take him home with me."

"If he belongs to someone, they sure don't take very good care of him," another boy observed.

"He's too nice a dog to let him starve or get hit by a car," Freddy continued.

"Sure, he's a neat dog," said a skinny kid in a cowboy hat. "But you know Mr. Turner won't let him ride the team bus."

Everyone laughed at that, and the chubby boy said gleefully. "Can you play shortstop, pooch? We could use one of those."

"That's not funny, Joey," the boy in the cowboy hat objected. "I'm the shortstop on this team, and he's just a dog." The boys giggled.

"He's a lost dog," said Freddy, "a dog that needs a friend."

"Are you going to keep the dog?" Joey wanted to know.

"I would if I could get him home," Freddy said.

The boys nodded. "But you can't get him home," one of the boys reminded him.

Freddy looked thoughtful. "Maybe I could if I had a little help from you guys," he decided.

"Forget it," said Joey. "You'd have to keep him hidden through the whole game."

"He could stay in the locker room," said Freddy.

"Oh, sure," snorted the shortstop. "Why, we'd never even get him on the bus."

"Yeah," another agreed. "Mr. Turner won't let anyone on the bus until he gets here. I think he'd notice if a dog came up the steps."

Freddy shrugged. "You never know until you try," he said.

The other boys looked at each other, considering this thought. Joey spoke up. "We'll get into an awful lot of trouble if we get caught," he said.

"Right," the redhead agreed. "But if we pull this off, we'll have something to talk about for a long time."

The other boys began to grin. "It would be kind of a neat trick," the boy in the cowboy hat admitted.

"Then, here's my plan," Freddy said excitedly. "Now listen carefully because we haven't got much time to make it work."

Seven

WHILE the rest of his troops scattered to make preparations, Freddy lured Barkley to a spot behind a dumpster. There they were close enough to the bus without being seen.

Before long he heard Mr. Turner calling, "Come on, guys. It's time to leave." The heavy-set man walked by Freddy and the dumpster. "All aboard for Wilson Junior High," he called.

Climbing into the driver's seat, the man adjusted his rearview mirror and called again. "Come on, guys. Get the lead out." But his team continued to amble slowly across the parking lot as if they had all the time in the world.

Then Joey rushed out from the restaurant to the bus. His chubby body showed a picture of concern. He banged on the driver's window frantically. He talked with his hands and babbled something that made no sense.

Mr. Turner tried to motion Joey around to the open door. He cupped his ear and shook his head, but the boy refused to budge. At last the driver opened his window and growled, "What's the problem? I can't understand a word you're saying."

"Gosh, Coach. You've got to help me," Joey pleaded. "I don't know where I left it."

"Left what? I can't help you if you don't make sense," the coach said.

Joey gulped and nodded. "It's my wristwatch. It's really valuable, and you've just got to help me find it!" he cried.

"Well, where did you last see it?" the coach asked.

When Freddy was sure that Joey had Mr. Turner's attention, he used a piece of hamburger to lure Barkley to the bus. There the rest of the team helped shield the dog from their coach's sight. Freddy headed quickly for a backseat. The Schnauzer followed the food in Freddy's hand without hesitation. As soon as Barkley was out of sight, the redhead signaled the boy in the cowboy hat. That boy was standing right behind Mr. Turner so that he could signal Joey to wind up his act.

The chubby boy reached into his pocket and smiled stupidly. "Gee," he marveled. "My watch is right here. I must have taken it off when I washed my hands."

Mr. Turner groaned. "Oh, for Pete's sake, Joey. Just get on the bus," he said. He slammed the window and waited impatiently for Freddy's friends to find seats next to him. Then he started the engine and put the bus in gear.

As soon as Barkley realized they were moving, he tried to get onto the seat above him. He was so determined to see where he was going that it took both Freddy and Joey to keep him down on the floor.

Mr. Turner noticed flying elbows in his rearview mirror. "What's going on back there?" he asked suspiciously.

"Joey pushed me," Freddy complained.

"Did not," answered Joey. "He just won't give me enough room."

"If you hadn't eaten so much, you wouldn't need so much room," Freddy said.

"Never mind," the coach demanded. "Knock it off, or I'll make you both sit in the front."

The boys nodded solemnly. Freddy felt under the seat to check on Barkley. At first the dog wiggled around a lot, but after a while he lay quietly. Finally, he began to snore.

They had been traveling for over an hour when the redhead happened to look down again. This time he didn't see the dog. A pair of furry ears popped up in the seat ahead of him.

"Kyle," he whispered desperately to the boy in the cowboy hat. "Kyle, do something!"

Kyle glanced around to see Barkley sitting there in plain sight and gasped. He quickly yanked off his big cowboy hat and stuffed it down over the dog's ears. Barkley's feet skidded out from under him and he fought to get back up.

Mr. Turner looked back just then and called. "You in the cowboy hat, sit up."

Frantically Kyle yanked the hat down over Barkley's eyes. The dog scrambled onto the seat again.

"That's better," said the coach. "Now you guys settle down back there because we're getting into some traffic."

Barkley could see out the window now in spite of the hat. They were in the city, his city. The bus was heading toward Elm Street. He moved his head back and forth excitedly. His tail celebrated while three boys did their best to keep him seated.

Suddenly the bus lurched to a stop. A truck blew its horn. "Ruff!" said Barkley.

When the bus was moving again, Mr. Turner glanced back. "Who said that?" he grumbled.

A boy toward the front coughed loudly. "It was me, Coach," he managed. "I've been getting a cold all week."

"We're almost there," Freddy whispered to the

cowboy hat, "so please behave." By now Barkley didn't have much choice because Kyle's hand was clamped shut over his muzzle.

Soon the bus pulled up at a big brick building and Mr. Turner went in. "Hey, Freddy," someone called from the front. "What are you going to do now?"

"You'll see," he called back. "Just hand me one of those equipment bags."

The other boys shook their heads. They handed Freddy a bag full of bats and balls. "You're crazy," said one. "That dog won't stand for it," said another.

"Sure he will," said Freddy, trying to convince himself. Dumping everything out of the sack he urged, "Come on, guys. We haven't got much time."

At once Kyle yanked his hat off the Schnauzer. Joey helped him hold the dog down as Freddy brought the sack closer. Barkley's warning growl made the rest of the team crane their necks. The dog was still interested in food. So while he gulped a hamburger, the boys got the sack over his head.

Just then someone hollered, "Mr. Turner is coming."

"Oh, no," squealed Joey, dropping the sack.

Barkley had no trouble escaping from the remaining two boys. He whirled and ran to the door just in time to scoot between the legs of the surprised coach.

Already out the door, Barkley heard Mr. Turner bellow, "You kids will be the death of me yet!"

Barkley was delighted to be in his hometown again. He sped around the side of the brick building and across the baseball field. A group of players doing warm-ups yelled, "Come here, dog. Want to play catch?" But Barkley kept going. He had to find Jamie. He had a lot of city to get through first.

Leaving the ball field, he darted down an alley, and then onto a quiet street. There were more alleys and more streets ahead. Some of the streets were lined with battered garbage cans and ragged-looking people. One scruffy character threw a bottle at Barkley that shattered against a nearby wall. The dog bounded away in terror as the man laughed.

On and on Barkley ran until he came to a street too busy to cross. Here the sidewalks were so full of people that he was forced to a slow trot. He looked down the alleys and saw trucks being unloaded. The people ahead of him kept stopping to stare in the shop windows. Barkley could barely make any headway. At last he began to walk in the street whenever there was a gap in the cars.

Suddenly a small white truck zoomed up to the curb and stopped. Barkley stiffened as the two men who got out started in his direction. One man carried a net of some kind. The other carried a long pole with a loop on the end.

"Hi there, doggie," said the man with the pole. "Wouldn't you like to come with us?"

Eight

BARKLEY took one look at the two men and their equipment and ran. But where could he go? he wondered. The street was full of cars. The crowd and a solid wall of buildings had him hemmed in. Shoppers tripped over him, tried to pet him, or drew back in fear. He could hear the little truck start up. It was following him.

Coming to a corner, Barkley saw his chance. He darted down a less popular street where he broke into a gallop. Before he had reached the middle of the block, he saw the little truck coming toward him. He couldn't understand how it had gotten there so fast.

Barkley doubled back, wishing he'd never left the crowd. Barkley noticed there was a truck coming from that direction, too. There was only one break in the wall next to him, and he took it. He dashed through a brightly lit door and found himself in an enormous room with a little food stand right in the middle of it. The smell of cigarettes and popcorn was so strong he started to sneeze.

"Hey," yelled someone from the food stand. "Get that dog out of here." Several people started toward Barkley. As he edged away, he saw the men from the trucks charging through the front door.

Frantically the dog raced around the room looking for a way out. He saw that one door led to someplace very dark. He thought it looked like a good place to hide. But things were so dark inside that he ran right into a cement column. In spite of the pain, he managed to stay quiet and wait to see what would happen next.

Suddenly music blared and one whole wall lit up into a moving picture. Barkley cringed in terror until he saw there were many rows of people watching the giant TV.

Then he heard voices outside the door. "We've got to catch him before he bites someone," a voice insisted.

"At least wait until intermission," urged another. "I don't want to upset my customers.

"Is there any way he can escape from here?"

"No. All the doors are shut except for this one."

"Okay, we'll wait for intermission."

Louder voices came from the men on the screen. "Mr. President," thundered a tough-looking army man. "Giant rats are invading the country."

Barkley decided to have a look around. For one thing, he needed to find an escape route. For another, the smell of popcorn was driving him crazy.

Sniffing his way between seats, he spotted a cardboard barrel full of the fluffy stuff. It was sitting right on the floor. The people next to it were too involved in the movie to eat.

Cautiously Barkley crept forward. He grabbed a mouthful of popcorn and retreated. The corn was heavenly, oozing with butter, warm and crunchy. He had to have more. No one paid any attention when he got his second mouthful so he was slower to leave this time.

"The rats are taking over the White House," said the movie. "We can't stop them, sir." A mixture of frightened "oooos" and "aahhhhhhs" went up from the audience.

As Barkley moved in for his third mouthful of popcorn, a hand touched his ear. "EEEEEEK," squealed a girl. "There's a rat in here," she shrieked, leaping to her feet. In her hurry to leave, she kicked over the popcorn and almost fell on Barkley.

The Schnauzer was frightened so badly that he ran blindly, bumping into people as he went. "Help," screamed a young boy. I'm being attacked."

Other voices joined him in panic. "I felt one, too!" "There are rats in here! Let me out!" "Wait

POPCORN

for me!" Suddenly the dog was in the middle of a stampede.

About that time the screen went dark and the ceiling lights came on. "Ladies and gentlemen," a voice boomed. "Please stay calm. Take your seats. There is nothing to be afraid of."

But no one was listening to the announcement. Instead, people were rushing to the exits. When Barkley realized there was a second door out of the building, he headed for it.

It wasn't easy to move in the mass of frightened people, so Barkley crawled under seats most of the way. When he got closer to the door, he had no choice but to join the mob. Several people stepped on him, and their piercing cries hurt his ears.

Dodging through the door at last, he looked around cautiously. When no one paid any attention to him, he breathed a sigh of relief and started on his way. He knew Elm Street was getting closer.

Barkley was tired after all his excitement. He

didn't get far that night. Instead he settled for a hard bed under a parked car.

* * * * *

Trotting through a little park the next morning, he saw two bicycles approaching. The boys riding them looked about Jamie's age, and his tail wagged hopefully. Neither of them looked familiar, and they passed without a word.

Then one of the boys stopped and looked back. "Hey," he cried excitedly. "Did you notice that dog back there?"

"What about him?" asked the other boy, also braking.

"That could be the dog we heard about, the one Mike Brewer is trying to find," he said.

"You mean the one that used to belong to Jamie Boggs?"

"Right!" shouted the first boy, whirling his bike around. "Come on."

Barkley glanced back to see the boys pedaling

at top speed toward him. He figured they wanted to tie him up, and he couldn't allow that. Quickly he galloped off, following the hedge that lined the park. With a burst of speed he dived through a small break in the shrubs and made his escape.

The Schnauzer continued to gallop for a long time after that. He wanted to reach Elm Street today for sure. Unfortunately he was getting hungry again. Every garbage can he passed was a temptation.

He managed to keep going until his nose detected something special. The smell seemed to be coming from a group of shiny cans in a yard with a high wire fence around it. Of course, the idea was to keep dogs out, but someone left the gate open.

Coming closer Barkley decided the can on the right was the one with the goodies. His tingling nose told him leftovers, maybe even steak. He looked around carefully and weighed the danger. If someone caught him in the enclosed area, he would be trapped, he knew. He sniffed the breeze and listened. There was no sign of life coming from the big house closest to him. Oh, the smell of that food! Barkley thought.

Edging nervously through the gate, Barkley nudged the lid off the can on the right. It clattered to the ground with a terrible racket. The dog leaped out of the gate ready to flee. But no one came. He crept back to the can and looked in. Ripping open the plastic bags inside he found a tremendous feast of bread, French fries, and steak.

Throwing caution to the wind, the dog knocked over the garbage can. He gobbled the food as fast as he could and made a terrible mess.

Suddenly the gate slammed shut. A voice cackled, "Aha! Caught you this time."

Backing out of the garbage quickly, Barkley saw an old man in baggy pants twirling a club in his hand. In one desperate motion the dog tried to leap the fence. The man was too fast for him. The club bounced off Barkley's head, then blackness.

Nine

WHEN Barkley woke up he was still in the fenced-in yard with the garbage cans. Things looked fuzzy. His head hurt horribly. Two men were looking at him.

"Good work," said the elegant-looking man in a suit. "You caught the scoundrel at last."

"Thank you, sir," answered the old man in the baggy pants. "Have you thought about what to do with our prisoner?"

The man in the suit shrugged. "Call the proper authorities, I suppose. There must be a number in the phone book," he said.

"Probably so, sir, but I have another suggestion," the old man said.

Already turning to leave, the man in the suit

looked surprised. "Really? What other options do we have?"

"Well, if I might say so, I have a friend who would take the dog," he said.

"And what would your friend do with him?" the other man asked.

"Henry knows a research lab that pays good money for strays. He could use the money, sir."

The man smiled a cruel smile. "Indeed? After the trouble and expense this dog has caused, I think that would be quite fitting." Then, starting back to his big house, the man added, "Yes, Justin. Tell your friend to come and get the dog."

"Very good, sir," called the other man. In a softer voice he sneered, "Hound, you're going to make old Justin some money. When those research people get through with you, you'll wish you'd left Mr. Blackburn's garbage alone."

Barkley waited until the man had gone before he struggled to his feet. His head still hurt. The food he had gobbled so fast was making him sick to his stomach. But he knew he had to try to escape before something worse happened.

He launched himself at the wire gate, but it didn't give an inch. His teeth were useless against it. Digging out was impossible. The ground was too hard, and his paws were already tender. At last he lay back panting and discouraged.

Then Barkley thought he heard voices. They sounded like children playing. He scrambled to his feet and barked softly. The voices came closer. He barked a little louder, hoping Justin wouldn't hear him.

Two girls appeared from behind some trees. They were pedaling their bikes slowly as if they were looking for something. They spotted Barkley.

"There he is," gasped a dark-haired little pixie. "It's the right dog. I'm sure it is."

"But what's he doing inside that fence?" wondered her pig-tailed companion.

"It looks like he's been eating garbage. Yuk," she said.

The girls lay their bicycles down and hurried

over to the fence. "He sure looks miserable," the girl in pigtails observed.

"Yeah. Let's get him out of there," said the dark-haired girl as she knelt beside the fence.

"Do you think we should?"

"Why not?"

Barkley was dancing excitedly by the gate now, his aches and pains forgotten. He wanted the girls to hurry and set him free. But a harsh voice stopped the dark-haired girl in her tracks.

"You there. What do you think you're doing?" Justin demanded. He was running toward them now with his club.

The girls froze in terror. "There's been some kind of a mistake," the pixie managed to say. "This dog belongs to a friend of ours."

"Mistake nothing," croaked the man. "That's my dog, and this is private property so get away from there."

"But we've been looking for a brown Schnauzer for days . . . " the girl in pigtails began.

"I don't care what you've been looking for,"

Justin snarled. "I say this is my dog. Now beat it before I use this club on you."

Frightened, the girls hurried to pick up their bikes and wobbled nervously away. Still, they kept glancing back at Barkley and frowning.

When Barkley saw his rescuers leaving, his spirit was crushed. His mournful howl could be heard for blocks.

"Quiet, you," bellowed Justin, "or I'll give you another taste of this club." That made Barkley stop howling immediately. Miserably he dragged his aching body to the far corner of the yard and lay very still.

Before long a battered, old pickup truck chugged up and stopped. A man with a bushy black beard got out and hurried forward. He was carrying a gun.

Justin ran to meet him calling, "Ah, Henry. I see you got my message. Say, what's the gun for?"

"It shoots darts," the newcomer said proudly. Then, checking the gun's sights, he added, "It'll put the mutt to sleep so he can't bite us."

"You and your toys," snorted Justin. "This club is all I need to put a dog to sleep. Be sure that gun comes out of your half of the profits."

"My half? It's me who takes all the chances. The least you can do is split expenses."

Justin shrugged. "I've got the dog. Do you want him or not?" he asked.

The bearded man thought for a minute. "All right," he agreed. "You get your usual amount, and I pay for the gun. Now let's get on with it."

Henry circled the fence until he had Barkley clearly in his sights. But, before he could pull the trigger, the fast-moving Schnauzer dived to a new position behind the garbage cans.

"Rats, I can't get at him," growled Henry.

We'll have to take those garbage cans out," Justin decided. "Keep me covered while I get them."

His friend agreed, and the two men moved to the gate. As he opened the latch Justin said, "Now keep a sharp watch because you might get a shot at him when I move this." Quickly he pulled away Barkley's protection, yelling, "Shoot, shoot."

"Ping," went a dart as it bounced off a can. Henry grunted with disgust.

"You're way too slow for this," Justin complained. "And watch where you aim that thing. You almost got me instead of the dog."

He was about to pull away a second can when a car suddenly screeched to a stop behind Henry's pickup. It was a black and white sedan with a big red flashing light on the roof. Following the car were a group of kids on bikes.

"There he is, officer," cried a dark-haired little girl. "That's the man with the big stick."

"Yipes," gasped a boy with glasses. "The other man has a gun."

A surprised Henry sputtered, "It only shoots darts." Then he and Justin quickly backed out of the gate, fastening it behind them.

"Hello, officer," Justin said warmly. "I'm very glad to see you."

The policeman's eyes narrowed. "Why is that?" he asked.

Justin forced a nervous little chuckle. "It's this dog, officer," he explained. "My friend here has had nothing but trouble with the animal since he first bought him. Now as you can see, he's made a mess of these garbage cans. Would you be so good as to help us catch him?"

"A few minutes ago he told us the dog belonged to him," the little girl with pigtails protested.

"He was lying then and he's lying now," the dark-haired girl agreed.

"And you were trespassing and butting into my business," snapped Justin.

"This dog belongs to Jamie Boggs," said the boy with the glasses.

Justin shot the boy a hard look. "Prove it," he snarled.

Ten

FROWNING, the policeman walked over to where he could see Barkley more clearly. "No tags, eh?" he muttered.

The children watched silently. The dog wagged his tail and whined, wondering why no one would let him out of the fenced-in area. Henry whispered something to Justin, but Justin shook him off.

Finally the policeman asked, "Is there any way you kids can prove your story?"

The children looked at each other desperately. "We could call Jamie Boggs," one of them suggested.

The policeman frowned some more. "Nope," he decided. That would still be one person's word against another. We need proof."

The little girl in pigtails was near tears. "Mike," she whispered, "you've got to do something."

Nodding, the boy with glasses walked over to the fence. He reached inside. Barkley moved up flat against the wire to have his ears scratched. "Officer, this dog knows me," said Mike. "Doesn't that prove something?"

The policeman sighed and shook his head. "All that proves is that he's friendly. Does the dog you're looking for know any tricks?"

"You mean like shaking hands or rolling over?" the girl in pigtails asked.

"Yes," said the policeman. "Something like that could be used as evidence."

The children were all thinking. "I've got it," squealed the dark-haired girl. "It's not exactly a trick. But remember what Jamie's dog used to do when he got fed?"

"Of course," Mike said excitedly. "I need some food."

"What is this?" growled Justin. "You kids are wasting my whole day. Next you'll want to send out for lunch."

"That won't be necessary," the policeman said coldly. Then, reaching into the front seat of his squad car, he produced a sandwich from his very own lunch. He handed it to Mike and said, "Now tell me what it is that I'm supposed to watch for."

"Well, sir," Mike began. "Jamie's dog, Barkley, begs for his food."

"Big deal," scoffed Justin. "Lots of dogs know how to beg."

"But they all do it a little differently," Mike insisted. "Barkley tips his head to the left, raises his right paw, and barks just once."

The policeman smiled at last. "That sounds pretty specific," he agreed. "Let's see what happens."

So everyone moved around toward the gate of the fence. The policeman helped Mike inside. Barkley had already spotted the sandwich so he met the boy eagerly. Dancing around with his

nose in the air, the dog tried to reach the food. But Mike held it away from Barkley.

Everyone held their breath as they waited to see what the dog would do. But Barkley was too excited. He just kept running around wagging his tail and whining.

Mike stood absolutely still, waiting for the dog to settle down. Then he said carefully, "Barkley, please listen to me. Are you hungry?"

Suddenly the dog realized what Mike was saying. His mouth burst into a happy grin, and he sat. Eyes sparkling, he cocked his head to one side, then he slowly raised his right paw. "Ruff," he said firmly.

A cheer went up from the kids watching. The policeman grinned and handed Mike a rope to use as a leash. The kids cheered again when the boy led Barkley from the fence.

"Well," said the policeman. "Barkley Boggs has spoken, and dogs never lie." Then he noticed Justin and Henry trying to sneak off. "Don't go away," he told them sharply. "I have some questions to ask you about some missing dogs in this neighborhood."

Before long a procession of bicycles set off for Elm Street with Barkley in the lead. He pranced and tugged at the rope Mike held, urging everyone to hurry. As they approached the Boggs' old house, he barked frantically. He bounced up and down, trying to tell Jamie that he was home.

But the dog soon sensed something was wrong. New flower pots hung from the porch. None of Jamie's things were lying in the front yard. A strange woman appeared from behind the house.

"Oh, you found the missing dog," she said kindly. "Sorry, pooch. Jamie isn't here."

Barkley's whole body drooped with defeat when Mike put him in his bicycle basket. "I know you're disappointed, fella," the boy told him. "But you'll see Jamie soon. I promise."

* * * * *

Jamie was sitting by the phone when Mike called. Mike told him the story, and Jamie leaped to his feet yelling, "You found him? You really did? Mom, Dad, they found Barkley! Come quick!"

His shout brought Mr. and Mrs. Boggs. "When? Where? Is he all right?" they demanded.

"He's fine," Jamie assured them. "But how are we going to get Barkley to Indiana? Will he have to be shut up in a cage again?"

Mr. Boggs smiled and shook his head. "Leave that to me," he said confidently. "The airline was pretty upset about this whole mess. I think they're ready to do something special for us."

Early the next morning Mike and his family and half the kids in the neighborhood took Barkley to the airport. When the unhappy Schnauzer saw where they were taking him, he actually groaned. He refused to look at anyone, and he had to be dragged from the car.

This time, no one tried to put him in a cage. He didn't even have to go into the crowded main building. Instead, Mike and Barkley got on a very small plane waiting for them. The pilot himself helped Barkley into a special seat belt that allowed him to look out the window.

Several hours later the little plane touched down with a gentle bump and coasted up to a lone building. Three people stood outside the building waving. And, as they got closer, the smallest person looked more and more like Jamie. It *was* Jamie!

Suddenly Barkley got so excited that the seat belt could barely hold him. "Easy, boy," Mike said, laughing. "We're almost there." But the dog got more and more excited. It took both Mike and the pilot to get his seat belt off. When someone opened the plane's door, he hurled himself through it and knocked Jamie right off his feet. The boy couldn't even get up because he was being licked to death, but he didn't care. Jamie just hugged his dog and cried tears of happiness.

Mr. and Mrs. Boggs shook hands with Mike.

They tried to pretend they weren't crying, too. "Good to see you, Mike," said Mr. Boggs, wiping his eyes. "How was the trip?"

"It was super," bubbled Mike. "When I grow up, I'm going to be a pilot."

At last Jamie managed to get up, and went

over to Mike. He was still hugging Barkley. "Gee, thanks, Mike," he sniffed. "I was afraid I'd never see Barkley again."

"I didn't exactly find him," Mike admitted, looking at his feet. "Some other kids were the first ones to spot him."

"But you spread the word that he was missing," Mrs. Boggs pointed out.

"And you helped to rescue him," Mr. Boggs added.

"Barkley had a lot to do with that," Mike said, blushing and scuffing the toe of his shoe.

"Well, I say you are a hero," Jamie decided. "And we're going to have a really great time while you're in Indiana. What do you say, Barkley?"

"Ruff," Barkley agreed.